To all my family, past and present
—M.S.

For my grandmothers, whose beautiful
stories enriched my sense of wonder
—A.A.

When Lola Visits

Text copyright © 2021 by Michelle Sterling

Illustrations copyright © 2021 by Aaron Asis

Library of Congress Control Number: 2020936277

ISBN 978-0-06-297285-9

The artist used gouache and digital to create the illustrations for this book.

Typography by Rachel Zegar

21 22 23 24   PC   10 9 8 7 6 5 4 3 2

❖

First Edition

When Lola Visits

Story by Michelle Sterling

Art by Aaron Asis

KATHERINE TEGEN BOOKS
An Imprint of HarperCollins Publishers

How do I know summer is here?

Summer smells like stone fruit ripening on the kitchen counter and jasmine on the bloom everywhere in the neighborhood.

Like my baby brother finger-painting out on the deck,
and like trouble brewing on a day of absolutely nothing to do . . .

It smells like mango jam simmering on the stove—
the first thing my lola makes after she flies in for her summer stay.
It smells like the sampaguita soap she uses:
a scent both familiar and far away.

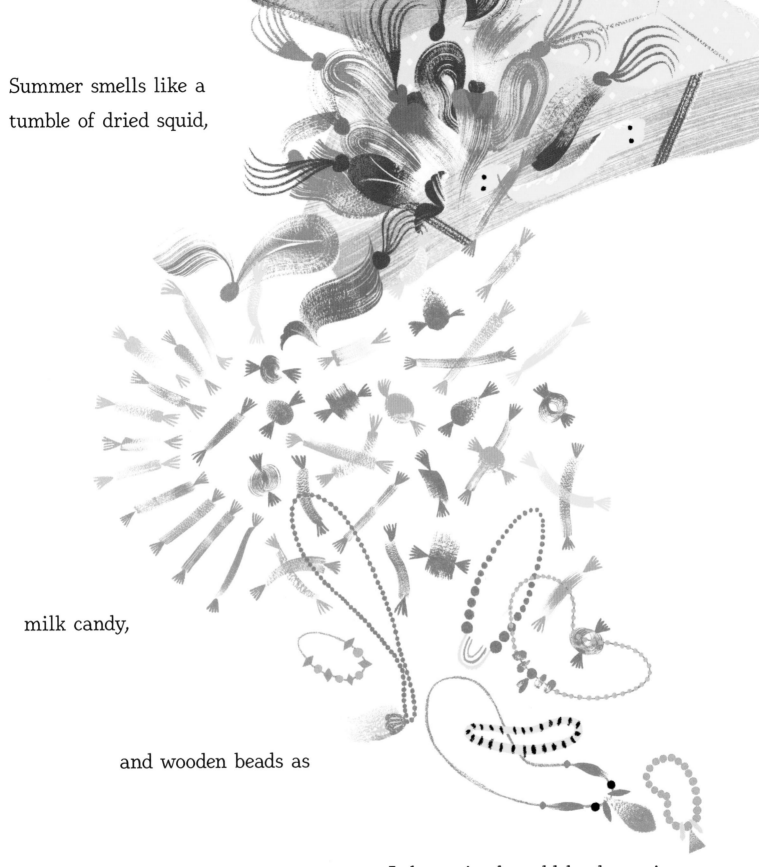

Summer smells like a
tumble of dried squid,

milk candy,

and wooden beads as

Lola unzips her old leather suitcase.

It smells like cassava cake covered with smooth and glossy custard, sliding out of the hot oven

as Lola tells us a story about the first time Mom made this cake and confused the sugar with salt.

It smells like chlorine from a million swimming lessons at the pool,
like blue silence when I'm finally able to float by myself
for the first time ever.

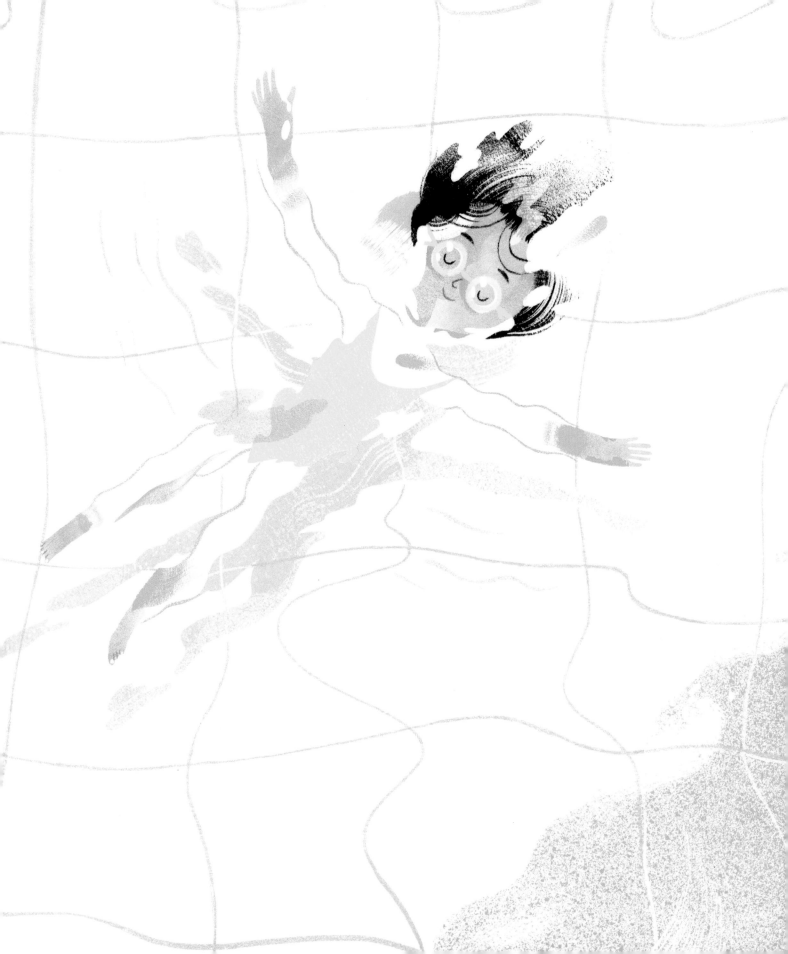

Summer smells like a freshly opened can of tennis balls to bounce against the side of the house

and gooey sunscreen and salt-soaked swimsuits at the beach.

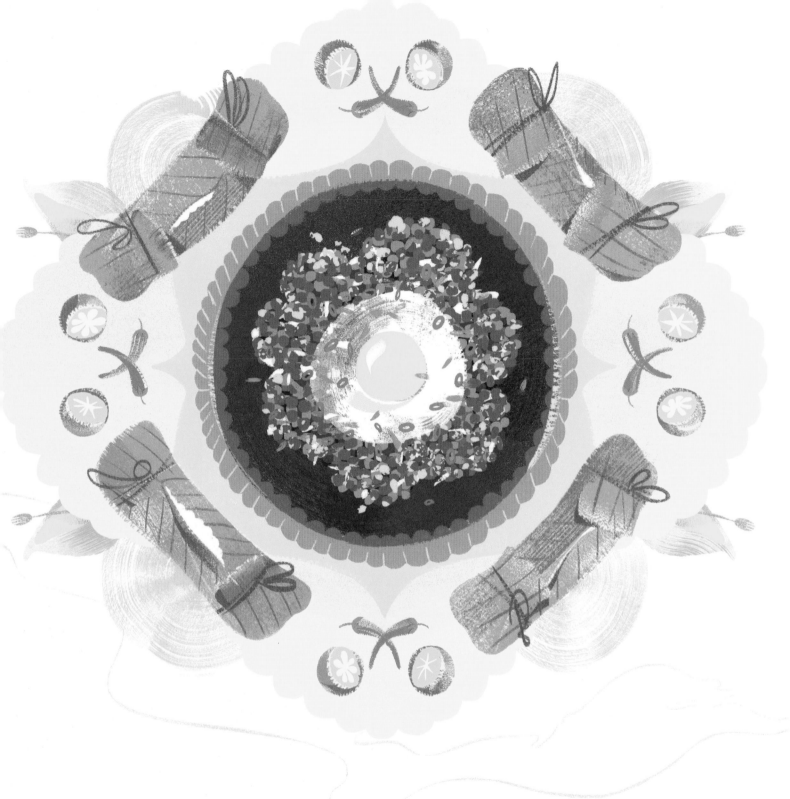

It smells like suman steaming on the stove for afternoon merienda
and tiny red chilies spilling into sizzling sisig as Lola lets me stir,
reminding me to scrape the flavorful bits off the bottom of the pan.

Summer smells
like standing under
crisscrosses of tree
branches with an apron
full of small golden limes.

Like kalamansi pie
and fireworks on the
Fourth of July.

It smells like rolling hundreds of lumpia and mixing together pinches of garlic and sharp vinegar.

Like warm banana leaves being laid onto the table for . . .

Kamayan.

Summer smells like the earliest hours of morning,
our lines cast into the lake.

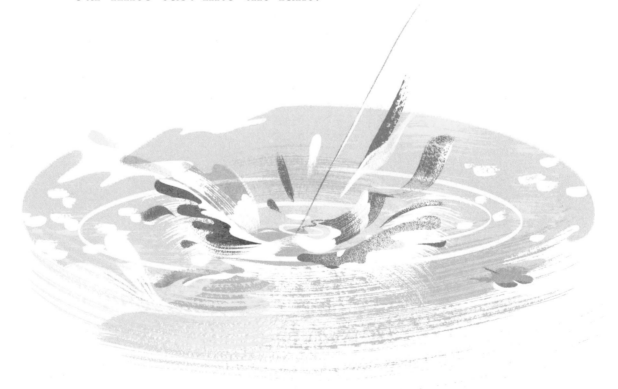

Smells like we just caught dinner!

Summer tastes like stuffed milkfish and brown-sugar
bananas grilling on a balmy evening,
just like Dad always ate when he was a kid.

It smells like an unexpected,

warm,

sticky

summer rain

and getting drenched while saying goodbye to Lola at the airport.

Our house is a little grayer without her soft, sweet
singing in Tagalog and Ilocano.
And the bitter melon tastes extra bitter in
tonight's dinner—not like how Lola makes it at all.

It feels like chilly bits of evening blowing
through the kalamansi trees.
Leaves are starting to pile up in the spot where
Lola used to sit next to me.

Summer smells like a letter to Lola
sealed in a mint-flavored envelope,
with bubblegum-scented ink,

wishing that I had a bowl of her arroz caldo to settle my butterflying stomach.

Summer feels like the last golden hour of the day drifting into an indigo night.

And it smells like melting cherry ice cream cones
as we race our scooters around the block one last time . . .

Until finally it smells like freshly sharpened pencils,
a stiff new backpack,
and the last sweet bits of summer—
in Lola's mango jam.